MW00886874

Meet You In Your Dreams

Written by Hope G. Forman

Illustrated by Dmitry Fedorov

1st Edition

Hope Bound Press - Los Angeles

2020

First paperback edition November 2020
Illustrations by Dmitry Fedorov

Print-ISBN: 978-1-7352223-0-1
E-Book- ISBN: 978-1-7352223-1-8

www.hopeforman.net

Dedication

This book is dedicated to the beautiful Georgia Veach and her loving parents, Chad & Julia, who are a shining example of faith, grace, joy, and strength, despite the obstacles life has thrown their way.

There once was a boy named Ryder,
whose world was about to grow wider.
He started out in just a family of three,
along with his playful pet puppy.

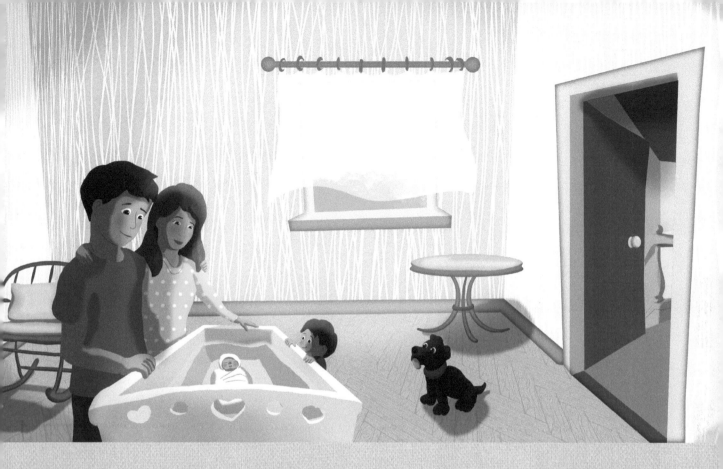

Until mommy's belly began to grow, grow, and grow,
and soon a baby girl was nestling in their home.

All eyes were on sister, for she was gentle and fair,
with skin soft as feathers and wavy brown hair.
She was thoughtfully named Seraphina
and all were pleased with her demeanor.

But there was soon another reason people looked baby's way,
with looks that peered beyond her lovely face.
For though her body grew, her mind did not
and speaking became a puzzle she couldn't unlock.

After many trips to the doctor and not much getting better,
the doctor dolefully said, "She may live with this forever".
Seraphina was then confined to a special chair,
causing others to look on, often choosing to stare.

Upon whispers and cries, from his own mother's eyes,
Ryder began to wonder, often asking "Why?"

At his sister he would stare, wondering all her secret thoughts.
He'd place flowers in her hair, braid by braid, lock by lock.

And every night, in sister Seraphina and little Ryder's room,
mommy and daddy would sit, crowned by the light of the moon.
They'd say nighttime prayers, tucking them under the covers,
reminding them each of their love for the other.

And every night, just the same,
mommy would assuredly say,
"Goodnight my Seraphina, I will meet you in your dreams,
where we can talk and dance and fly with angel wings."

When all was quiet and Ryder's eyelids quite heavy,
he sometimes caught sister, eyes closed, with a grin, wide and steady.

Then one day from school, Ryder came running, his eyes in tears and nose all runny,

"Mommy! Mommy! The kids all said, "Seraphina isn't normal, but different and funny.""

"My sweet sweet muffin", his mother replied,

"not everyone can see a person for what's on the inside.

What matters most is the love that we show
and that we always always hold onto hope.
Perhaps Seraphina isn't like all the others,
but know this, my love, *you* are her big brother.

Whether or not she can speak,
she can still hear and she can still see.
Your daddy and I decided long ago,
we would not give in to fear in our home.

Be strong my dear Ryder, she looks up to you.
Your life will be richer for having loved her too."

But one night was different, before Ryder fell asleep;
he repeated the words his mother would often speak,
"Goodnight Seraphina, I will meet you in your dreams,
where we can talk and dance and fly with angel wings."

The next morning, he awoke with the memory of a dream,
but it felt more real than any other thing!
He sat and pondered all the wonder he'd explored,

from oceans to mountains and midnight skies they soared!

He and Seraphina, together, hand in hand,
danced around, discovering all the land!

They rode cotton candy clouds and unicorns backs.

They even got to share all their favorite snacks!

They swam with dolphins and whales through oceans and seas.

They ran with cheetahs and tigers and climbed the tallest of trees.

But what Ryder cherished most, above any other thing,
was when he and Seraphina shared their wildest of dreams.
And never before that moment, had Ryder discovered,
such joy than that of Seraphina calling him "big brother".
It was then that Ryder realized, deep down inside,
what they shared could, somehow, surpass space and time.

Then in a moment of stillness what came hovering from above,
were two dazzling angels with golden wings and eyes of love.
Without saying a word, yet with smiles warm and tender,
they tossed sparkling dust for each child to remember,
that no matter what things looked like, on the outside,
they'd always have their dreams, to journey through the night.

When Ryder was fully awake and recounted all he'd seen,
he went to Seraphina's bed to quietly watch her dream.
But what Ryder saw then came as quite a surprise:
Seraphina looking at him with a grin and locked eyes.
She then opened her fist to reveal: a secret held inside;
it was sparkling dust, from their adventure through the night.

THE END